Lacey's Dancing Shoes

By Alexandra Reid

Designed & Illustrated by John & Anthony Gentile,
Louis Henry Mitchell and Joe Schettino

HarperFestival®
A Division of HarperCollins*Publishers*

Ivy Rose and Lacey were starting ballet classes at the Wingdom Royal Dance Academy. Before the first class they bought matching leotards and ballet slippers.

They bought matching tights and even matching hair ribbons. "We're best friends," said Lacey to the saleswoman.

At the ballet class Ivy Rose and Lacey stood next to each other at the barre.

"I'm nervous," whispered Lacey.

"I hope the teacher isn't mean," whispered Ivy Rose.

Just then the teacher came in. "Let's begin," she said,
clapping her hands. "Please bend your arms like this and plié."
All the girls copied the teacher. "Good," she said.

"Now let's try something more difficult. Girls, please fly up and come down gracefully."

All the girls flew up in the air and came down gracefully, except for Lacey, who landed with a thud.

"Lighter, Lacey," said the teacher. "Pretend you're a feather." Lacey blushed.

"Now, girls, pirouette in the air." All the girls twirled and whirled, but Lacey twirled in the wrong direction and bumped into Sea Crystal.

"Ouch!" said Sea Crystal.

"Sorry," said Lacey.

On the way home Lacey burst out, "I'm terrible! I'll never be able to dance!"

"Lots of the other girls made mistakes too, Lacey," said Ivy Rose. "Moon Shimmer kept beginning her leaps on the wrong foot. And Sea Crystal kept forgetting to bend her elbows."

Lacey smiled.

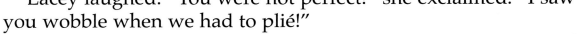

"Anyway," Ivy Rose continued, "you can't expect to be perfect with only one lesson. Not like me."

Lacey laughed. "You were not perfect!" she exclaimed. "I saw you wobble when we had to plié!"

"Exactly," said Ivy Rose. "You'll get better. It just takes practice."

But at the next class Lacey wasn't any better. In fact, she was even worse than before! She was so nervous about making a mistake that she couldn't concentrate on what the teacher was saying. She kept using the wrong arms and legs. She kept turning the wrong way and bumping into the other girls.

And when the teacher told them to jump up in the air and hover motionlessly, Lacey jumped so high she bumped her head on the ceiling! At the end of the class she flew out of the room in tears. Ivy Rose flew after her.

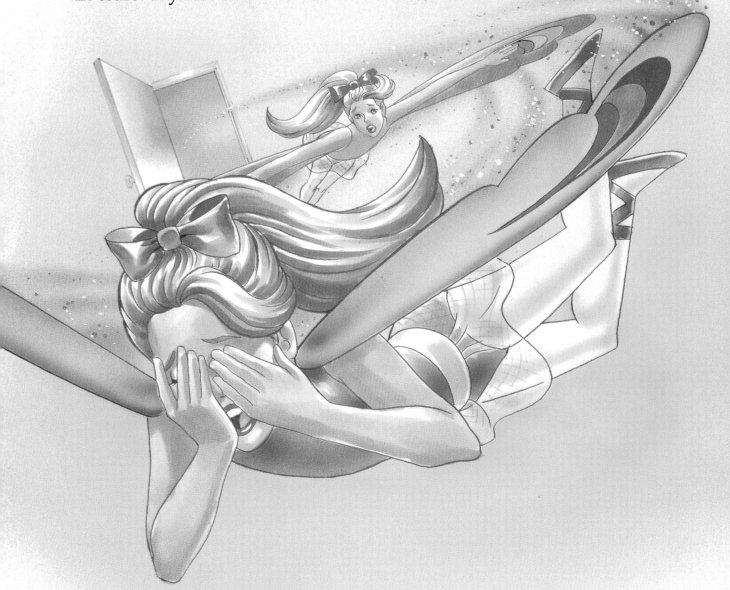

"I'm quitting!" said Lacey. "I'll never be able to dance, so why even try?"

"Dancing is really hard work," said Ivy Rose. "You have to practice and practice. Even professional dancers practice every day."

"But I'm just naturally bad at it!" said Lacey.

"The only thing you're being bad at is not believing in yourself!" said Ivy Rose.

Lacey was so surprised that she stopped crying. "Of course you're making mistakes," said Ivy Rose. "If we knew how to dance already, we wouldn't be taking lessons! Why don't you come over to my house tomorrow with your pointe shoes and we can practice in between classes? Now stop complaining and let's go get some Sky Cones."

The next afternoon Lacey flew over to Ivy Rose's house. Slowly Ivy Rose and Lacey went through all the steps they had learned in class. Lacey wasn't scared to make mistakes in front of her best friend, and she even began to dance some steps better than Ivy Rose!

"You see?" said Ivy Rose. "You believed you could dance and look what happened. Just practice every day and you'll see how well you can dance. It's all up to you!"

"If it is to be, it's up to me! Thank you, Ivy Rose!" Lacey hugged her friend and danced her way home.

Lacey practiced every day, every chance she had. She pirouetted in her bedroom, and leapt and twirled her way to dinner. She pointed her toes when she was doing her homework, hovered motionlessly when she was reading, and even pliéd while she brushed her teeth!

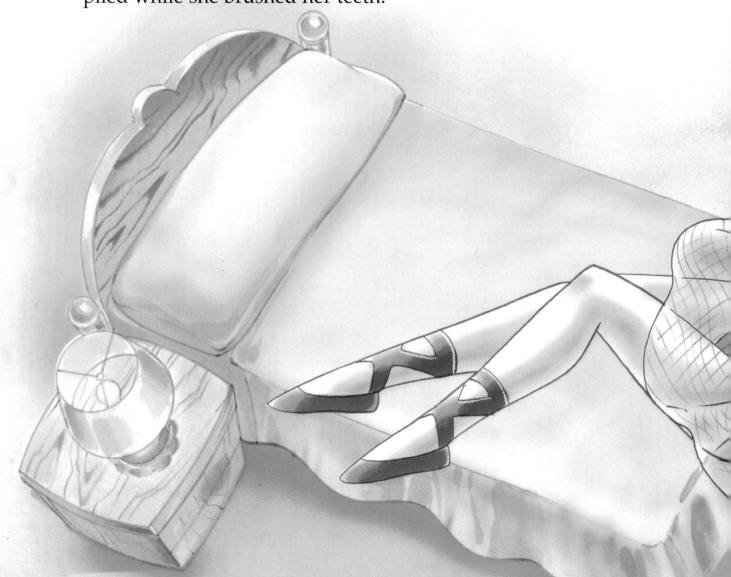

When the next dance class arrived, Ivy Rose asked Lacey, "Are you still nervous?"

"Not anymore," said Lacey. "Because I know I can do it if I want to. And I don't have to be perfect. I just have to do my best."

Lacey's best was terrific! And even when she tripped at one point, she didn't mind. She picked herself up, grinned at Ivy Rose, and kept right on dancing.

After that class Lacey just got better and better. In fact, when the class put on its end-of-the-year performance, she was picked to be one of the lead dancers!

"See what a little practice does?" said Ivy Rose just before they went onstage.